WHERE THE GOOD LUCK WAS

WHERE THE GOOD LUCK WAS

by
OSMOND MOLARSKY

illustrated by
INGRID FETZ

HENRY Z. WALCK, INC.   NEW YORK

Molarsky, Osmond
  Where the good luck was; illus. by
Ingrid Fetz.   Walck, 1970
  64p. illus.

  Story of four city boys who try to
raise money to buy a pair of aluminum
crutches for a friend.

1. Cities and towns - Fiction
I. Illus. II. Title

THIS MAIN ENTRY CATALOG CARD MAY BE REPRODUCED WITHOUT PERMISSION.

WHERE THE GOOD LUCK WAS

The day Arnold McWilliams got out of the
hospital his three best friends were sitting on
his front stoop, waiting for him to come home.

"How come you're walking on crutches?"
Jackson said. "We thought you were all cured."

"Yeah," said Rudy and Kevin. "How come?"

"I have to walk on crutches at least three
months," Arnold said. "My ankle got broken
good."

"Next time maybe you won't parachute off a garage roof with an umbrella," Rudy said.

Kevin said, "How come you're using those old wooden crutches? How come you don't have some of those shiny crutches made of aluminum?"

"How come you don't have a shiny new bike with four-speed gearshift?" Arnold asked.

"Because it costs too much."

"Right. The hospital lent me these wooden crutches, but aluminum ones cost twenty-four dollars and fifty cents," Arnold said.

"That's a lot of loot," Rudy said.

"That's why I don't have them. Anyway, who needs them? Watch this." Arnold swung his feet up in front, then up in back and galloped off at full speed to the corner. Then he spun around and galloped back again. "I've got the fastest crutches in the West," he said. "Anybody want to race me?"

Nobody wanted to race him. They were all thinking.

Finally Kevin said, "Arnold should have shiny aluminum crutches."

"Why?" Rudy asked.

"Because he should," said Jackson. "A kid on our block with aluminum crutches—that would be cool."

"Hey, yeah!" Kevin agreed. "How would you like aluminum crutches, Arnold?"

"That's okay with me," Arnold said.

"Let's start an Arnold McWilliams Aluminum Crutches Fund and get him a pair," said Kevin.

"Maybe we could get some used ones and shine them up," said Rudy.

"No!" said Jackson. "New ones! They've got to be new!"

"How do we get the money?" Rudy asked.

"Easy," Jackson said.

"Easy how?"

Jackson thought a while. Then he said, "How do I know? Why did you have to spoil it?"

"Sorry," Rudy said.

Just then Lucky came tearing around the corner, carrying a long stick. Lucky was always finding things. Once, a long time ago, he found a brand-new Boy Scout knife. After that, he always walked with his head down, to be sure he wouldn't miss anything valuable on the ground. As a result, he usually had bumps on his forehead. But he found an earring that looked like gold, a belt buckle, a new pair of white shoelaces, a ballpoint pen, a pair of glasses and a total of eighty-seven cents.

"What's up, Lucky?" said Jackson. "What are you doing with that long stick?"

Lucky didn't answer Jackson's questions. "Who's chewing gum?" he wanted to know.

"No one," said Rudy. "Why?"

"You know the drugstore, corner of Fillmore and Ashbury?"

"Yes."

"You know the sidewalk grating, in front of the store?"

"Yes."

"I saw a quarter down there! A quarter! It wasn't there yesterday, either!" Lucky was excited. "With a wad of gum on the end of this stick, I could snag it. Who has gum?"

Jackson said, "I have a piece in my pocket. For three cents, I'll chew it and let you use it."

"Three cents!" said Lucky. "For a nickel I could get a whole pack!"

"You don't have to pay me till after you snag the quarter," Jackson said.

"Wait a minute," said Kevin. "We're starting a fund to buy Arnold aluminum crutches. How about if Jackson donates the gum and Lucky donates the quarter?"

Lucky looked at Arnold, who was galloping around on his crutches like a wild mustang. "What's wrong with wooden crutches?" Lucky asked.

"He's got to have aluminum ones," said Jackson. "A kid on our block with real aluminum crutches—it would be cool."

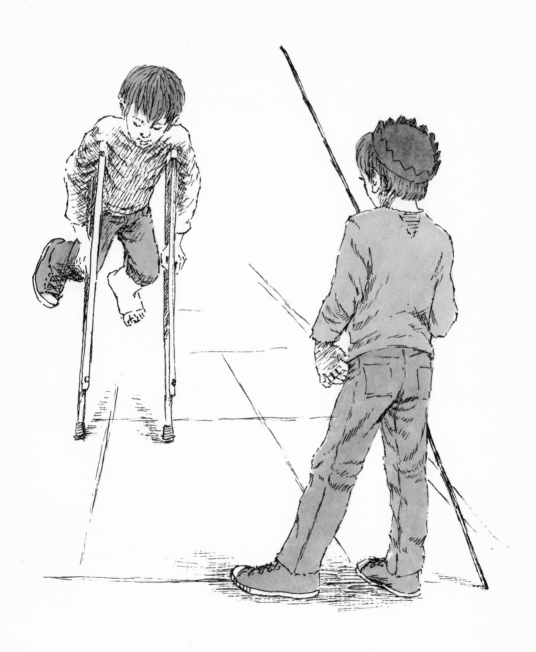

MEADE PARK ELEMENTARY SCHOOL
LEARNING CENTER

Lucky tried to think of a reason against aluminum crutches, but he could not think of one. "Okay," he said, finally. "I'll donate the quarter if Jackson donates the gum."

Jackson popped the gum into his mouth and began to chew it, as Lucky led the way to the lost quarter.

"Where is it?" Rudy asked.

"Down there," said Lucky. They all looked down through the grating, and there was the quarter, shiny and new and plain as day.

"You know what?" said Kevin. "I bet there's a hundred gratings around here. We could get money for the fund out of all of them."

"That idea is groovy," Jackson said. Then everyone agreed the idea was groovy and they would do it.

"That gum is chewed by now," Lucky said. "Let me have it."

"Not till I get the flavor out of it," Jackson said. "I'm only donating the gum—not the flavor."

Finally, when Jackson had chewed out all the flavor, he put the gum on the end of Lucky's stick. Lucky began to poke the stick down through the grating. His aim wasn't very good and he had to make many tries before he finally touched the quarter with the gum. He pressed down on it, to make it stick. But when he

pulled the stick up the quarter dropped off before he could get it through the grate. Lucky felt the gum. It had gotten hard and no longer was sticky. "Gum gets hard too soon after you chew it, unless it's really hot out," he said. "We'll have to wait for summer."

"By that time Arnold won't need the crutches," Jackson said. "There must be some way of getting it out."

"I've got it," said Kevin. "Rudy, give me your magnet." Rudy reached in his pocket and handed his magnet over to Kevin. "Who's got a piece of string?" Kevin asked.

"Here," said Jackson, and in a minute Kevin was letting the magnet down on the end of the string. The string was too short, and everybody groaned.

Kevin untied his right shoe, took out the shoelace and tied it to the end of the string.

"Good thinking," Jackson said.

Slowly Kevin let the magnet down. At last it touched the quarter. Everyone cheered.

Kevin began to pull the magnet up. Nothing stuck to it except a rusty nail that had been lying next to the quarter. Everyone groaned again.

"That's funny," said Rudy. "The quarter didn't come up."

"Boy, are we stupid," Kevin said. "I just remembered—magnets pick up iron and steel. A quarter isn't made of iron or steel. No wonder it didn't come up with that old nail. That nail is made of iron."

"We better start thinking some more," Jackson said.

"There has got to be a way to get money out of gratings," Kevin said. "There has to be a way." He thought and thought. "My mother's vacuum cleaner!" he said all of a sudden.

"Right," said Rudy. "We can put the hose down there and suck up the quarter. Not only that, we can go around sucking up everything down in grates, trash and all. Then we sort out the treasures. We'll have aluminum crutches for Arnold in no time."

Everyone agreed that this was the best plan yet, and off they went to Kevin's house to get the vacuum cleaner. Kevin's mother was working, so there was no problem about getting it.

Back at the grating, they realized they had no place to plug in the vacuum cleaner. They were standing outside the drugstore, wondering what to do, when they heard a voice. "You can use *our* electricity."

The boys looked up and saw Charlotte Tinsley leaning out of a window. Charlotte lived in the apartment over the drugstore. She was letting down a string.

"Tie the vacuum cleaner cord to the string, and I'll pull it up," she said.

Jackson tied the cord to the string, and Charlotte pulled it up a little way. "Do I get a nickel if you get the quarter?" she asked.

"No," said Jackson.

"Then I won't plug in the cord."

"The quarter is for the Arnold McWilliams Aluminum Crutches Fund," said Rudy. "Everybody is donating things. We'll let you donate your electricity."

"Oh," Charlotte said. "That's different," and she pulled the cord up the rest of the way and plugged it in.

"This is going to be mellow," Kevin said, as the motor started up. But when they tried to stick the hose down through the grating, they found it was too big. And this time they were really stuck. No one could think of a single thing to do. Dozens of gratings were full of money and treasure and there was no way at all of getting it up.

"Maybe we could get a stork with a long beak and train him to peck down through the grating and pick up stuff."

"Maybe we could borrow a big snake from the zoo and let it down by the tail and teach it to pick up treasures in its mouth."

As the boys were thinking and making foolish suggestions, along came old Mr. Murdock B. Pendleton. He walked past the boys, stopped suddenly and turned around and looked at them. "What are you boys doing with that vacuum cleaner?" he asked.

"We were going to suck up treasure from the grating," Lucky said. "But it won't work."

"Treasure, eh?" said the old man.

"We need it to buy aluminum crutches for Arnold McWilliams. That's Arnold McWilliams there. He broke his ankle parachuting off a garage with his mother's umbrella."

Arnold swung his feet up in front, then up in back, then galloped up to the corner and back again.

"A noble enterprise," said the old man. The boys didn't know what he meant, but they didn't ask him. "How would you like to earn a little money for your fund?"

"How would we earn it?" asked Rudy.

"I'll tell you," said the old man. "My attic is full of things I want to throw away. Old newspapers. Old magazines. Old clothes. Old books. Old junk of every kind. It's a waste of space and a fire hazard up there. I want it out, and I'll pay you fellows thirty-five cents an hour for carrying it down and putting it on the side-walk for the garbage collector."

"Do each of us get thirty-five cents an hour?" Jackson wanted to know. "Or is that for all of us?"

"Thirty-five cents an hour for all of you," the old man said.

"Wait a minute," said Jackson, and he drew all his friends together and they whispered for a minute or two. Then he said, "We have a union, and we're striking for twenty-five cents an hour for each of us."

"Twenty," the old man said.

Jackson drew his friends together again and

whispered, then said, "Okay. When do we start?"

"Right now. Come with me."

"Not me," said Lucky. "I'm going to stay right here and snag that quarter. There's got to be some way of doing it."

"Good luck, Lucky," said Kevin, and off they went after the old man.

Walking briskly, Mr. Murdock B. Pendleton led the boys three blocks to the north and two blocks to the east, then to the middle of the block. Arnold galloped along on his crutches at a good clip. When he got too far ahead, he stopped to swing his feet up in the air, front and back.

The houses on the old man's block were big and tall and covered with fancy stuff. Some had a round tower at one side, like a castle. Fanciest of all was the house of Mr. Murdock B. Pendleton. The boys had often seen it, but none of them had ever been inside.

"Here we are," said the old man. He took out his big key ring, found the right key and let them into the house through the tall front door. He led them up the winding staircase past the second floor, to the third floor. There he opened a door that led to a straight and narrow stairway to the attic. "Up there," he said.

"You go first, Rudy," Jackson said.

"Let Kevin go first."

"Okay," Kevin said. "Who's scared?" He started up the stairs, followed by Rudy and Jackson. Arnold, on his crutches, thumped up behind them.

Suddenly, there they were, in a huge, cold, musty room. A little light came from two small windows, at the front and the back, and they could see that they were right under the roof of the big old house.

Stacked up all over were old furniture and piles of newspapers and magazines. There were boxes with writing on them that said BOOKS, MARTHA'S WEDDING DRESS, PETER'S FOOTBALL TOGS, YALE '09, ROBERT'S HOCKEY SKATES. And a small box was marked RAGS. Why would anyone keep a box of rags, Kevin wondered. He picked it up and thought it was very heavy for a box of rags.

Cobwebs hung between the roof beams and the walls, and the boys could write their names in the dust that covered everything. When they began to move around, the dust got into their

noses and made them sneeze. And the more
they sneezed, the more dust they stirred up.
This work wasn't going to be easy, and they
hardly knew where to begin.

Jackson called down the stairs to Mr. Murdock B. Pendleton. "Hey, we can't carry down
that dresser or that big chair."

"Never mind those. Begin with the newspapers and magazines."

The bundles of papers and magazines were heavy. Rudy took out his knife and cut the strings, and they divided the bundles into smaller bundles. Arnold supervised as the others went up and down the stairs, like ants, carrying armloads of old newspapers and magazines and piling them out on the sidewalk. Working all together, they cleared out the attic of odds and ends in less than two hours.

"That makes me feel good," Mr. Murdock B. Pendleton said. "That makes me feel much better. How much do I owe you?"

Jackson looked out the window at the clock in the church steeple. "We started at two o'clock," he said. "Now it's five minutes to four."

"Let's call it two hours," the old gentleman said. "At twenty cents an hour for three boys, that makes sixty cents for each hour. Two hours is a dollar and twenty cents."

"There were four boys," said Jackson.

"I'm not counting the one on crutches. He didn't carry anything." He took two dollars out of his billfold and handed it to Jackson. "Can you give me change from two?"

The boys had no change.

"I'll tell you what," the old man said. "Take that vacuum cleaner you carry around with you and go back up to the attic and clean up some of that dust. I'll make it two dollars flat."

Another eighty cents toward the aluminum crutches, the boys thought.

"We'll do it," Jackson said.

When they finished, the old man gave them the two dollars. Jackson was appointed treasurer of the Arnold McWilliams Aluminum Crutches Fund and put the money in his pocket.

"Now all we need is twenty dollars and fifty cents more," Jackson said. "Hey, Kevin, how're we going to get it?"

Kevin didn't answer. He was thinking.

"Hey, Kevin!"

"What?"

"How are we going to get the rest of the money for the crutches?" Rudy asked.

"I don't know," said Kevin. "Listen, fellas. Remember that little box that was marked RAGS?"

"Yes," said Jackson.

"Why was it so heavy?"

"Maybe they were heavy rags," Rudy said.

"I'm going to look inside that box," Kevin said.

The RAGS box was still there on the sidewalk with the rest of the trash, waiting to be collected. The boys watched as Kevin opened it.

"Those are rags, all right," Jackson said.

"Rags can't be that heavy," Kevin said, and he reached in and pulled out a handful. The boys looked inside to see if anything was under the rags, and their eyes opened very wide.

"It's a black leather box."

"Lift up the lid."

"It has a lock on it."

"Shake it."

Kevin shook it. It was heavy, but it didn't make a sound.

Suddenly, among the rags, Kevin saw a very small key. He picked it up. "Look! The key to the lock! Let me try it!"

He was so excited that he couldn't put the key in the lock.

"Here, I'll do it," said Jackson, taking the key. He put it in the lock, turned it to the left and opened the lid. A look of disappointment came over their faces.

"I thought maybe it would be something valuable," said Rudy.

"So did I," said Jackson.

"It's nothing but some old knives and forks, and they're all black," said Arnold.

Bedded down in soft, purple velvet were rows and rows of knives, forks and spoons. The knives were all the same, twelve of them. But there were three kinds of spoons and three kinds of forks, a dozen of each. Kevin lifted out one of the spoons. It was a beautiful shape, and fancy initials were carved in the handle. Kevin looked at it carefully, then said, "Hey, Rudy, give me your magnet."

Kevin held the spoon against the magnet and let go of it. The spoon fell to the sidewalk.

"Maybe it's silver," he said. "A magnet won't pick up silver.

"My father has some silver coins," Jackson said. "They turn black like that spoon."

Kevin put the spoon back in its place in the box. "I wonder why it said RAGS on the outside box."

"Maybe to fool robbers," Arnold said.

"I polish up my father's coins with soda," said Jackson.

"Maybe if we polished up the spoons they'd be worth a lot of money," Kevin said.

"Maybe a hundred dollars. Maybe we could sell them," said Jackson. "And I know where. Down at Frisby's pawnshop. My mother sold her

watch at the pawnshop once. You can sell anything there."

"Let's go," said Arnold, and started to gallop
off on his wooden crutches.

"We can't sell them. They belong to the old
man," Rudy said.

"He threw them away," said Jackson. "It's
just like we found them. Finders, keepers. The
garbage truck would come and take them away."

"I think we ought to tell Mr. Pendleton,"
Rudy said.

"That's right," said Kevin. "I bet he wouldn't
throw them away if he knew. Let's vote on it.
Everybody for keeping the stuff and selling it,
raise your hand."

Jackson's hand shot up. When he looked
around and saw he was the only one, he slowly
pulled it down.

"All for telling the old man, raise your hand."

All four boys raised their hands.

Kevin picked up the black box and started
up the front steps. The others crowded after
him. They rang the old man's bell.

They waited. Nobody came. They rang again. "We can't wait here all day."

"We can wait a minute."

"Okay. One minute. One . . . two . . . three . . ."

Everyone started to count up to sixty. In less than twenty seconds they were up to forty.

". . . fifty-two, fifty-three, fifty-four . . ." Their minute was almost over. They were ready to leave fast. ". . . fifty-nine . . ."

The door opened. It was Mr. Murdock B. Pendleton.

"Yes?"

Kevin opened the box. The old man stared at the knives, forks and spoons. He took out a spoon and looked at the carved initials. "J. C. Julia Cook. My grandmother," he said. "This silver belonged to my grandmother on my mother's side."

"Did you mean to throw it away?" Jackson said.

"They were in a box with RAGS written on it, up in the attic," Kevin said. "We put the box out on the curb with the rest of the stuff."

"Boys," Mr. Murdock B. Pendleton said, "you have done me a very good turn. This silver is worth a great deal—especially to me. You deserve a reward." The boys watched, as he paced up and down the porch. At last he said, "How much do you think it should be?"

Suddenly a thought came to Jackson. "Twenty-two dollars and fifty cents," he said.

"That's an odd figure," the old man said. "But if that's what you want, that is what you will get," and he took out his billfold and counted out exactly twenty-two dollars. Then he reached into his pocket, came out with a handful of change and counted out exactly fifty cents. He wrapped up the coins in the paper money and held it out. Jackson took it and said, "Thank you."

"Let's go to the crutches store right now," said Rudy, "before we lose it or spend it," and away they went, with Arnold leading the way.

Inside the store, Jackson said to the clerk, "We'd like to look at a pair of aluminum crutches. They're for him," and he pointed to Arnold. Then he added, "We have twenty-four dollars and fifty cents," and he showed the clerk the money.

"Yes, indeed," said the clerk, and he brought out a pair of aluminum crutches and adjusted them to the right size for Arnold. "There you are, young fellow. Try them out."

Arnold walked up and down a couple of times. "They are nice and light," he said. "They're really cool."

Then he swung his feet up in the air, in front. He sat down hard. "Owwwwwww!" howled Arnold, and his friends picked him up. "That hurt," he said.

"What did you think you were doing?" said the clerk. "Crutches are not to do tricks on."

"Aluminum ones aren't. I can see that," said Arnold. "I'll stick to wooden crutches."

Everyone was disappointed. No boy on their block would have aluminum crutches. And what

would they do with the twenty-four dollars and fifty cents in the Arnold McWilliams Aluminum Crutches Fund?

"We could buy a secondhand bicycle and all of us use it," Rudy said.

"We could get in a taxi and drive all over the city," said Jackson.

"We could buy that big, huge cake with the bride and groom on top, in Bickerson's window," Arnold said.

But for some reason not one of them felt like
spending all that money on something foolish.
Arnold could see that his friends were disappointed and tried to think of how he could
make it up to them. Suddenly he thought of
something.

"Listen," said Arnold. "I've got an idea. These crutches I have—did you know they're not mine?"

"They're not?" said Rudy. "Whose are they?"

"Remember I told you the hospital lent me these until I get well. I have to give them back."

"They loaned them to you?" said Kevin.

"That's right. They've got plenty of crutches to lend. Only they have no aluminum ones."

"I got it," said Kevin. "We donate a pair of aluminum crutches to the hospital."

"Right," said Arnold. "Just what I was thinking."

"Cool, man," said Jackson.

"You haven't heard the half of it yet," said Kevin. "On the crutches, it could say *Donated by the Arnold McWilliams Aluminum Crutches Fund.*"

"You're really groovin'," said Arnold. "How do we put that on the crutches?"

"We can get a plastic name tape made at the Arcade, with sticky stuff on the back to stick it on. My daddy had one made for his fishing rod."

"Mellow," said Rudy. "How much does it cost?"

"A quarter," said Kevin.

They rushed back into the store. "We'll take the crutches," Jackson said, and gave the man the money. "Never mind wrapping them up."

Off they started with the new aluminum crutches, taking turns on them as they went. They were heading for the Arcade, to get the name tape made.

Suddenly Rudy stopped. "We have no quarter," he said. "We spent all the money on the crutches."

"Follow me," said Jackson. He turned left into Fillmore, and in less than two minutes they were in front of the drugstore where Lucky was still fishing through the grating.

"Hi, Lucky," said Jackson. "Any luck?"

"No," said Lucky. "I snagged the quarter okay. With bubble gum. It would even stick in winter. But I dropped my Scout knife down there and I can't get it up."

"Tough," said Jackson. "We made twenty-four dollars and fifty cents and bought the crutches already."

Lucky could hardly believe it. Twenty-four dollars and fifty cents! But there were the crutches right before his eyes.

"We need another quarter," Jackson said. "For a name tape. So we can donate the crutches to the hospital."

"You can't have the quarter," Lucky said. He had lost his Scout knife trying to get the quarter and now he wasn't going to give it up.

"Okay, then," said Jackson. "Rudy won't snag up your Scout knife with his magnet unless you let us have the quarter for the fund."

"Get the knife first," Lucky said.

Rudy got the magnet out of his pocket, unwound the string and borrowed Kevin's shoelace once again. A few minutes later, he pulled the knife through the grating and Lucky grabbed it.

"Thanks," he said. "My luck is sure with me." He handed over the quarter and walked away with his head down, looking for more treasures.

"Let's go," said Jackson. "Let's get the name tape made," and off they raced to the Arcade.

Kevin was the best speller, so he turned the dial to the right letters. The others took turns pulling down the handle. Gradually the tape came out. There it was. *The Arnold McWiliams Alumum Crutches Fund.* Kevin left one "l" out of Arnold's last name, and he spelled aluminum wrong, but that made no difference to the hospital. They were very glad to get such a valuable donation and gave the boys a letter of appreciation signed by the head doctor, the head nurse and several of the assistants. Altogether, it had been a lucky day—even for Lucky.

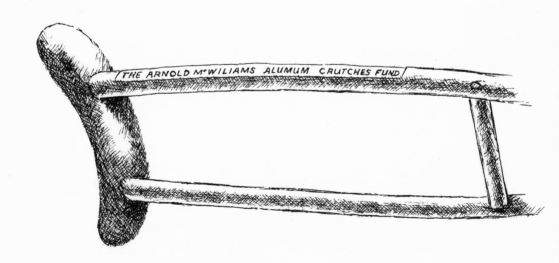